PLEASANT HILL
D0384508

Abracadabra!

Magic with Mouse and Mole

Wong Herbert Yee

Houghton Mifflin Company • Boston • 2007

FOR COLLEEN
AND THE BOOK BEAT

www.houghtonmifflinbooks.com

The text of this book is set in Adobe Caslon Regular.
The illustrations are charcoal pencil and gouache.

Library of Congress Cataloging-in-Publication Data
Yee, Wong Herbert.
Abracadabra! Magic with Mouse and Mole / written and illustrated by Wong Herbert Yee.
p. cm.
Summary: Mole is mad about magic until he takes his friend Mouse to a show that turns out to be all tricks, but then Mouse conjures up a special night program to show him the enchantment found in nature.
ISBN-13: 978-0-618-75926-2 (hardcover)
ISBN-10: 0-618-75926-3 (hardcover)
[1. Magic tricks—Fiction. 2. Nature—Fiction. 3. Moles (Animals)—Fiction. 4. Mice—Fiction.] I. Title. II. Title: Magic with Mouse and Mole.
PZ7.Y3655Abr 2007
[E]—dc22 2006034520

Manufactured in China
WKT 10 9 8 7 6 5 4 3 2 1

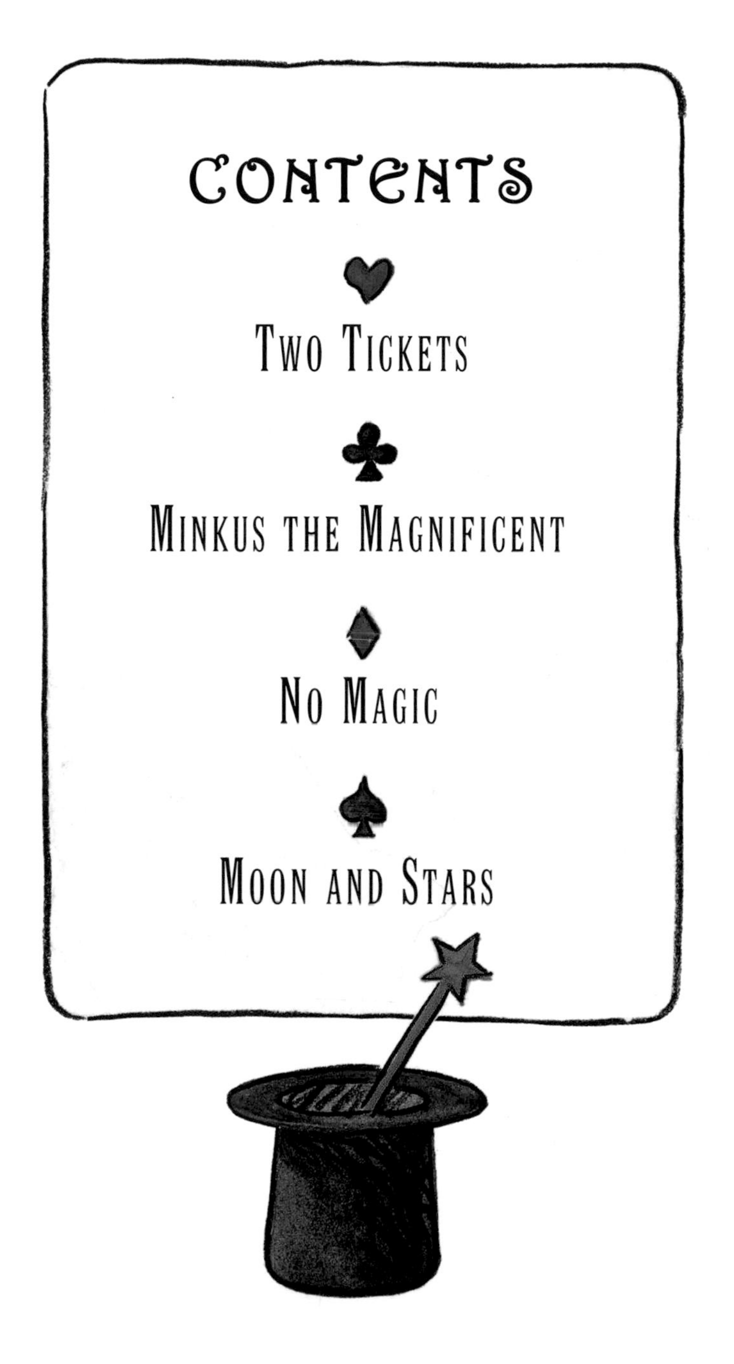

Contents

Two Tickets

Mole paced outside Mouse's house.

Mole tapped his foot.

Mole rubbed his snout.

He circled the oak tree three times.

Mole knocked on Mouse's door:

TAP-TAP-TAP.

"Come out, Mouse!" he called.

Mole circled the oak tree three more times.
He stopped under Mouse's window.
"Mouse, hurry UP!" he hollered.
"I do not *wish* to be late!"

In his paw were two tickets
for the magic show!
Mole was simply *mad*
about magic!

Mouse paced back and forth.

Mouse tapped her foot.

Mouse twirled her tail.

Two dresses lay on the bed.

One was purple with yellow polka dots.

The other was white with red stripes.

A third dress hung on the closet door.

It was black with moons and stars.

"Mercy," squeaked Mouse.

"How will I ever decide!"

TAP-TAP-TAP. Mouse heard Mole knocking.

"Just a moment!" she cried.

From her window, Mouse heard Mole calling.

"A minute more!" Mouse shouted.

She still could not make up her mind.

"Oh, well!" sighed Mouse.

She shut her eyes.

"Eeny, meeny, miny . . . MO!"

Mouse opened her eyes.

"Moons and stars

it will be!"

Rows of logs sat in front of a camper.

"See, we are *not* late," said Mouse.

"In fact, Mole — we are the first ones here!"

There were so many seats to pick from.

"Where should we sit?" Mouse wondered.

"Up front," said Mole.

"Maybe I can *snag*

an autograph."

In a few minutes, all the seats were taken.

“A full house!” Mole clapped.

“House?” said Mouse.

“Where is the roof?

Where are the walls?”

“Do not be silly, Mouse,” said Mole.

“That is just *show biz* talk.”

The door to the camper swung open.
A white rabbit in a checkered vest hopped out.
"Tickets, tickets, please!" he called.
When all the tickets were collected,
the rabbit went back into the camper.

BAM! The door was kicked open once more.

Out came the rabbit, dragging a table.

Snap, snap, snap, snap went the legs.

Back inside went the rabbit.

He returned moments later

with a tablecloth.

FWOOMPH!

The white rabbit flipped

the cloth high in the air.

It floated gently down,

covering the table.

"Ladies and gentlemen!"
announced the rabbit.
He waved a paw at the camper.
"Introducing — MINKUS . . .
the Magnificent!"

POOF!

A cloud of smoke filled the air.
"Eek!" squeaked Mouse.
PLOP! Mole toppled right
off the log!

Minkus the Magnificent

♣

The white rabbit had vanished.

In his place stood the magician.

"Bravo!" shouted Mouse.

"Bravo!" yelled Mole.

Everyone began to clap and cheer.

Minkus the Magnificent swept

off his top hat.

"Welcome, magic lovers!" he crowed.

The magician wore a ruffled shirt.
A long black cape hung on his back.
Minkus the Magnificent lifted his arms.
Mouse giggled. "He looks like a giant bat."
"Shush," Mole scolded.

"As you can see," said the magician,
"there is nothing in my right paw *or* my left."

Minkus made a fist and tapped it with
his magic wand.
"Abracadabra!" he cried.
Something green poked out of his fist.
Mouse nudged Mole.
"What is *'abracadabra'*?"
"Do not be silly," whispered Mole.
"That is just more *show biz* talk."

"A volunteer?" asked the magician. *"Moons and Stars!"* he said, pointing to Mouse. Minkus held his fist out. *"Pull!"* said the magician.

Mouse gave the cloth a tiny tug. "Eek!" she squeaked. The green cloth was attached to a blue one. *"Again!"* ordered Minkus.

Mouse yanked on the blue cloth.

A red one came next.

Mouse pulled and tugged,

and pulled some more.

Before long, she was

knee-deep in fabric.

Minkus untied the last cloth. It was orange.

"For you, *Moons and Stars!*"

"Bravo, Mouse!" yelled Mole.

Everyone began to clap and cheer.

Next, Minkus took out a deck of cards.

He fanned them across the table.

"A volunteer?"

asked the magician.

Mole eagerly

stepped forward.

"Pick a card," said Minkus, "ANY card!"

Mole paced back and forth.

Mole tapped his foot.

Mole rubbed his snout.

He circled the table three times.

Finally, Mole selected a card.

He held it so everyone but

the magician could see,

then hid the ace

underneath the others.

Minkus shuffled the cards.

He invited Mole to cut the deck.

The magician tapped the deck with his wand.

"Presto, CHANGE-O!" he cried.

Mole stole a peek at the card on top.

"How did you do that?" he gasped.

Minkus winked. "A magician never tells!"

He signed the ace of clubs for Mole.

"Bravo, Mole!" shouted Mouse.

Everyone began to clap and cheer.

"And now . . ." barked the magician,

"the GRAND FINALE!"

Minkus took his hat off.
He set it upside down
on the table.

Next, the magician untied his cape.
He swirled it over his head and
covered the top hat with it.

Minkus the Magnificent swayed to and fro.
He waved his wand with a flourish.

"ABRACADABRA!" Minkus cried —

and jerked the cape off.

Two long ears poked out of the hat.

PLOP! Mole toppled right off the log.

The crowd went bonkers!

Mouse sprang to her feet.

"Bravo!" she squeaked.

"Encore!" cheered Mole.

The white rabbit stood to take a bow.

Suddenly, the table began to wibble-wobble.

"Yikes!" yelped the rabbit.

The table tipped —

then flipped upside down.

There was a HOLE

in the center!

Cards rained down on the crowd.

ALL were the *ace of clubs!*

"We've been tricked!" Mole hollered.

Everyone began to boo and hiss.

POOF! A cloud of smoke filled the air.

By the time it cleared, Minkus the

Magnificent had vanished!

"Rats!" muttered Mole.

He ripped his card in two.

Mole was no longer

mad about magic.

He was just *mad!*

No Magic

◆

Mouse knocked on
Mole's door: TAP-TAP-TAP.
Mole did not answer.
He was not at home.
Mouse skipped along
the path to the pond.
There was Mole sitting in his boat.
"Hey!" Mouse shouted.
Mole did not answer.
He did not even look up.

Mouse climbed into the boat.

"Are you still mad?" she said.

Mole let out a sigh.

He tossed a stone into the pond: PLOP!

"Yesterday I was mad; today I am sad."

Mole handed Mouse a pebble.

Mouse flipped it into

the water: PLIP.

"Why are you sad?" she asked.

Mole got out of the boat.

He found another pebble and stone.

Mole pitched them into the water: PLIP-PLOP.

"Yesterday there was magic," sulked Mole.

"Today there is *not*.

Minkus was *not* magnificent.

Minkus is *not* a magician.

Minkus is a FAKE!"

"But magic tricks are what magicians do,"
said Mouse. "It's just — *show biz!*"
"Tricks they may be," grumbled Mole.
"Magical they are NOT!"
Mole picked up two pebbles,
a stone, and a large rock.
He hurled them with
all his might:

PLIP,

PLIP,

PLOP—

PLUNK!

“I say *phooey* to magic!

Phooey to show biz!

There is NO such thing as *magic!*”

“Don’t be silly,” said Mouse.

She hopped out of the boat.

“See that caterpillar?” Mouse pointed.

“I see it,” grumped Mole.

“That caterpillar will form a *chrysalis,*”

she explained. “From the chrysalis,

a beautiful butterfly will fly.

That is no trick, Mole. *That* is magic!"

"How long will *that* take?" muttered Mole.

Mouse twirled her tail.

"Oh, a few weeks."

She waded into the pond.

"See those things swimming to and fro?"

"You mean the little fish with bulgy eyes?" Mole pointed.

"Those are *tadpoles*," said Mouse.

"*Soon* the tadpoles will sprout legs.
Soon the tadpoles will grow arms.
Tadpoles turn into *frogs*.
That is no trick, Mole.
That is *magic!*"
Mole rubbed his snout.
"How long does *soon* take?"
"A few months, perhaps," said Mouse.

Mouse and Mole watched the sun set.
They headed back to the oak.

Poink! An acorn plunked
Mole on the head.
"Ouch!" he cried.
"See that nut?" Mouse pointed.
Mole picked up the acorn.
"Who is being silly now?"
"*Someday,*" said Mouse,
"that nut will grow into
a magnificent oak!"

Mole gazed in awe up the tree trunk.

"How long is — *someday?*"

Mouse nibbled her tail.

"Ten years, I should think —

no rushing Mother Nature."

"TEN YEARS!"

exclaimed Mole.

"I need magic NOW!"

Mole jammed the acorn into his pocket.

He marched downstairs in a huff.

Moon and Stars

♠

TAP-TAP-TAP. Mole heard a knock at the door.

"Why, it's nearly midnight!" He yawned.

"I wonder who *that* could be?"

He crept out of bed

to investigate.

A sheet of paper had been

slipped under the door:

Mole ventured a peek outside.
Someone had set a stump in the yard.
Mole looked about. He sat down
on the edge of his seat.
"Tickets, tickets, please!" called a voice.
PLOP! Mole toppled right off the stump.
A white rabbit snatched
the paper and ran off.

He returned dragging a table.

Snap, snap, snap, snap went the legs.

Another rabbit, this one brown,

came by with a tablecloth.

FWOOMPH!

The brown rabbit

flipped the cloth

high in the air.

"It is midnight on the dot!" announced the rabbits. "Please welcome . . . *MOUSE the Marvelous!*"

Out stepped Mouse from behind the oak. She had on her moons and stars dress. The orange cloth was wrapped around her head.

Mouse carried a glass jar and wooden spoon.
She set the jar on the table.
It looked empty.
Mouse undid the orange cloth.
She laid it over the jar.
Mouse waved the wooden
spoon in circles.

"Eeny, meeny, miny . . . MO!"
She tapped the jar three times,
then yanked the cloth away.

The glass jar began to shimmer.

It grew brighter,

and brighter.

Mouse unscrewed the lid. The tiny lights flew up and into the night sky. "Thank you, fireflies!" Mouse waved. Mole rubbed his eyes in wonder. "Bravo, Mouse!" he cheered.

"A volunteer?" asked Mouse.

Mole looked to his left.

Mole looked to his right.

He was the only one there.

Mouse handed Mole a flashlight.

"Follow me," she said.

They stopped in front of a mimosa plant.

"Eeny, meeny, miny . . . mo," whispered Mouse.

She tapped the branch

with her spoon.

The fernlike leaves snapped shut.

Mole nearly dropped the flashlight.

"How did you do that?" he gasped.

Mouse winked. "A magician never tells! And now . . ." squeaked Mouse, "the GRAND FINALE!"

The two rabbits folded the table legs: *snap, snap, snap, snap.*

They tilted it up on end.

"As you know, Mole," Mouse began,
"there is a *hole* in this table."
She stuck her head
through the trapdoor.

"Do not be silly," said Mole.
"As you can see," continued Mouse,
"there is nothing in this hole."
"Except your head." Mole chuckled.

Mouse smiled. “WHO is being silly now?”

She hung the cloth back on the table.

The rabbits lifted the table over their heads.

They circled behind Mole.

“Pardon me,” said Mouse.

She stepped around the stump.

Mouse the Marvelous swayed to and fro.
She waved the wooden spoon with a flourish.
"Eeny, meeny, miny . . . MO!" cried Mouse.

Slowly, she drew the cloth aside
and pushed the trapdoor open.

PLOP! Mole toppled
right off his seat.
The hole had vanished!
In its place — *a full moon!*
"Bravo, Mouse!"
hollered Mole. "Bravo!"
Mouse took a bow. She thanked
the rabbits for all their help.

It was a *marvelous* summer night.

The moon above was *magnificent*.

Mouse stretched out on the tablecloth.

Mole plopped down beside her.

"You were right, Mouse." He yawned.

"There is magic after all."

Mouse nodded.

"Of course there is."

"Just remember, Mole. *Real* magic takes time.
Be patient; keep your eyes and ears open.
Magic is all around!"
But Mole's eyes were not open.
He was not listening either.
Mole was fast asleep.
Soon Mouse was too.
Together they slept,
beneath the moon
and stars.